Jean Gilder's
Second Picture Book

by Jean Gilder

THE MAY QUEEN

'I hope I am chosen to be May Queen!' thought Marigold. But Marigold's big sister, Daisy, won the votes by a narrow margin.

'Marigold, don't be sad!' said kind Daisy, 'You can be my best "lady-in-waiting"'.

Tiptoes the pony said she would pull the cart if she could wear ribbons too: so the teddies made her look very pretty.

Then Daisy sat on the throne on the cart, and was pulled by Tiptoes through the village.

Marigold threw sweets and flowers, and had just as many cheers as the May Queen did!

MRS TRUFFLE'S TEA-DANCE

Mrs Truffle and Gillie were working hard preparing for a tea-dance, which was to be held in the cottage garden.

'I wish Bobbie was able to help us,' sighed Gillie. But poor Bobbie had hurt his leg, and was lame.

The band arrived and began to play jolly music. The animals had tea, and some of them danced. Then Gillie saw that Bobbie had arrived. 'Let's have tea,' she suggested.

Suddenly Bobbie said, 'I would love to dance – come on, Gillie!' and soon he was skipping about, his bad leg quite forgotten!

THE VILLAGE FÊTE

Russell Rabbit was very proud of the marrow growing in his garden. In fact he was entering it in the flower and vegetable show; so he fed and watered it, and guarded it from hungry slugs.

The day of the show arrived. Russell cut the marrow and polished it – but, oh dear, it was too heavy to lift! It seemed he would never reach the show tent.

Just then Sally came by, pushing her baby in a pram. So Russell borrowed the pram and rushed down the hill – just in time to win first prize!

He didn't forget to thank Sally for her help!

THE BEACH BARBECUE

Lying in the shade on a hot summer's day, the woodland folk decided to dip their paws in a nearby pool – but it was quite dried up!

Then Biffa Bunny had an idea. 'Let's go to the seaside – it will be cooler there,' he suggested. So they loaded some food and drink onto a large cart.

The animals walked for a long time, getting more and more hot and tired. 'How much further?' grumbled Monty Mole. But over the next hill, they suddenly saw a stretch of sparkling blue.

'The sea, the sea!' they called.

How lovely it was! The animals ran down the beach and into the little waves that lapped the sandy shore.

When they felt cooler after their swim, they built sand-castles and played ball, and Badger flew his kite.

Soon Biffa had a good fire going, and a delicious smell of baked potatoes and sausages filled the air. How hungry they all were!

The day on the beach was such fun that the animals decided to stay for as long as it was sunny.

'After all, I think we *need* a good holiday!' said Biffa.

THE APPLE PIE DAY

One day, Dilla Rabbit found an old apple tree which had been long forgotten. She ran home for her husband. 'Hurry, William, and bring the wheelbarrow!' she shouted.

So, for the rest of that day, they picked pink and red apples, and took them home to cook. Dilla made pastry and William and his friends cooked the apple pies to a lovely golden brown.

Later, the animals sat at a long table in the evening sun, and ate apple pie and cream in great content!

LATE FOR SCHOOL

Babs and Bobbie Bunny were on their
way to school. 'Hurry, Bobbie, or we shall
be late,' called Babs.

But just then, elderly Meggie Rabbit trotted across the path, tripped,
and fell. Babs and Bobbie hurried to help her as she sat nursing her back
paw, squeaking with pain.

Babs tied her own clean hanky round Meggie's leg, while Bobbie
fetched Meggie's husband, who lived nearby. Between them they helped
Meggie home.

'Now we *shall* be late for school!' said worried Babs.

And they were!

Mr Brock said sternly, 'You are very late! After school, you must write one hundred lines – I MUST NOT DAWDLE'.

Babs and Bobbie were too timid to explain what had happened.

But just then Meggie's husband appeared at the schoolroom door. 'I just thought those two very kind little bunnies might get into trouble for being late – it was not their fault …' And he told Mr Brock what had happened.

'Oh well, that's different,' Mr Brock beamed happily, 'We can gladly forget about any work after school!'

TEDDIES' CHRISTMAS EVE

When Mummy Bear asked her son, Timmy, to look for the Christmas decorations, he couldn't find them anywhere.

'We must have thrown them away by mistake,' said Daddy Bear. 'Try Mrs Speckle's shop; perhaps she will have some for sale.'

But Mrs Speckle had sold out! Timmy wandered home sadly. Then he saw some coloured paper which had been thrown away.

Timmy spent the day making paper-chains and foil stars. Mummy Bear made sugar bells, and Daddy Bear gathered holly and ivy.

When Timmy's friends came round they thought the room looked grand!

BOXING DAY AT FERNDALE

Christmas was over, and the little village of Ferndale was quietly glistening under a light fall of snow.

Mr Brock, the schoolmaster, was missing his pupils. 'Hmm, much too quiet for ME!' he thought. 'I know, it's time we had a party – a *village* party – for the old folks as well as the youngsters!'

So he called on Babs and Bobbie Bunny's and they all spread the news of the party, to be held in the Village Hall.

The only one who couldn't come was Meggie Rabbit, who still had a bad leg from when she'd tripped over some time ago.

But Babs and Bobbie thought of a good idea. With Mr Brock's help, they tied some old skis to a chair, and were able to pull Meggie through the snow. 'Whee! This is FUN!' squeaked Meggie, who hadn't moved so fast for years!

The party was a huge success – the whole village was there, and everyone brought something nice to eat. The animals played games – hunt the thimble, blind-man's buff, musical chairs and lots more.

What amusement they all had, and when Mr Brock suggested they should have a party every year on Boxing Day the animals raised a cheer that echoed around the whole woodland!

... What fun musical chairs was!